It was the day before Christmas. Speckles and Dottie were decorating.

"I love the holidays!" Speckles barked as he hung a dog-bone ornament on the tree.

"Me, too!" replied his sister as she strung some sparkly lights.

The Dalmatian twins loved Christmas. Every year, they put up lots of ribbons and lights and bows so their house would look extra special for the holidays.

HOLIDAYS

A Very Merry Christmas

SCHOLASTIC READER • LEVEL 3
700-1500 WORDS

Puppy In my Pocket®

By Sierra Harimann
Illustrated by The Artifact Group

SCHOLASTIC INC.

New York   Toronto   London   Auckland

Sydney   Mexico City   New Delhi   Hong Kong

ISBN 978-0-545-28145-4

© 2011 MEG. All Rights Reserved.

PUPPY IN MY POCKET® and all related titles, logos, and characters are registered trademarks of MEG. Licensed by Licensing Works!®

Published by Scholastic Inc. SCHOLASTIC and associated logos are trademarks and/or registered trademarks of Scholastic Inc. Lexile is a registered trademark of MetaMetrics, Inc.

12 11 10 9 8 7 6 5 4 3   12 13 14 15 16/0

Designed by Angela Jun
Printed in the U.S.A.
First printing, September 2011   40

"Oh, no!" Dottie said. "I just hung the last strand of lights, and the tree is only half finished! I'd better go to the store for more."

"Don't be long!" Speckles replied. "I'll need your help getting that star on top of the tree."

Dottie realized there was one other thing she still needed to buy — a Christmas present for Speckles!

Maybe I'll see something perfect at the store, she thought.

"How lovely!" Dottie said when she saw the display in the store window. Then something special caught her eye. "That's it! I know just what to get Speckles!"

Dottie picked out a beautiful strand of sparkly red lights. She also chose a set of paw pads for skateboarding, just like the ones in the window. They were the perfect gift for Speckles!

"Is that all?" the sales puppy asked her.

"Yes, that's everything," Dottie said as she opened her purse.

The sales puppy told Dottie the amount.

"But I don't have that much!" Dottie said sadly, her tail drooping.

"I'm sorry," the sales puppy replied. "None of these items are on sale."

BUY and SELL

7

Then Dottie had an idea. She pointed to the sign on the counter.

"If I sell you my charm collar, will I have enough?" she asked.

"Yes, you would have plenty," the sales puppy told Dottie. "But that's a pretty collar. Are you sure you want to sell it?"

"I'm sure," Dottie replied. "I love this collar, but I really want to get my brother, Speckles, the perfect Christmas gift."

By the time Dottie got home, Speckles had finished decorating the rest of the tree.

"Great timing!" he barked happily. "We'll hang the last strand of lights, and then you can help me put this star on top."

"Ta-da!" Dottie exclaimed. "It looks terrific!"

"Hooray!" Speckles barked. "And I have just enough time to get to the store before it closes. I still have to do my Christmas shopping."

Speckles knew exactly what he was going to get
Dottie for Christmas — a new charm for her collar!

"They're all so nice, it's hard to decide," Speckles said as he looked at the charms.

Then one caught his eye. It was a Christmas tree made of sparkly red and green stones.

"I'll take that one!" Speckles barked happily.

"Good choice!" the sales puppy told Speckles. Then she told him how much it was.

"Oh, no!" Speckles replied sadly. "I don't have enough."

"Maybe you'd like a different charm?" the sales puppy asked. "Some of these cost less."

14

Speckles shook his head. "The Christmas tree charm is perfect," he told the sales puppy. "My sister, Dottie, would love it."

Then Speckles had an idea.

"I know just what to do!" he told the sales puppy.

"Mmmm!" Speckles said when he got home from the store. "Those cookies smell so good."

He reached out a paw for a cookie.

"Speckles, no!" Dottie scolded. "Those are for our Christmas party tomorrow!"

"Sorry," Speckles said sheepishly.

The next day, Speckles and Dottie greeted their friends Gigi, Spike, Montana, and Freddy.

"Merry Christmas!" Spike barked.

"Merry Christmas, Spike," Dottie replied as she took Spike's coat.

"Who wants some Christmas cookies?" Speckles asked.

"I would love some!" Montana replied.

The other puppies barked in agreement.

"Let's open presents!" Dottie said. "I can't wait to give Speckles his gift. I think he's going to love it."

"That's a great idea," Speckles agreed. He turned to Freddy and grinned. "I want to give Dottie her gift, too. It's perfect for her!"

The puppies all swapped gifts. Spike had a gift for Freddy, and Freddy had one for Spike. And Montana and Gigi had gifts for each other, too.

First, Gigi and Montana opened their gifts.

"*Oh, la la!*" Gigi exclaimed as she saw the new charm collar. "I adore it! This is *très jolie*. That means *very pretty* in French."

"And I love my new scarf!" Montana told her friend. "Thank you so much."

Next, Freddy and Spike opened their gifts.

Freddy got Spike a brand new skateboard. And Spike got Freddy a PuppyPod music player.

"Thanks, Freddy," Spike barked. "You're a great friend."

"You, too, Spike," Freddy agreed. "What a cool gift!"

Finally, Dottie and Speckles gave each other their gifts. First, Dottie opened her package.

"Oh, Speckles!" she barked as she admired her Christmas-tree charm. "It's beautiful."

Then Speckles opened his gift. Dottie had bought him
paw pads for skateboarding.

"I know you're always scraping your paws when you
try new tricks," Dottie said. "I hope you like them."

"Thank you, Dottie!" Speckles said. "This is the perfect gift. But I have to tell you something. I sold my skateboard so that I would have enough money to buy your charm!"

"Oh, no!" Dottie cried. "I can't believe you sold your skateboard!"

"It's okay," Speckles said with a shrug. "I really wanted to get you something special."

"Me, too," Dottie agreed. "That's why I sold my charm collar to get your skateboarding paw pads!"

For a second, no one said anything. Then suddenly, Dottie and Speckles both began to laugh. Soon everyone else was laughing, too.

"I think I can help," Gigi said. "Dottie, you can have my sparkly rhinestone collar so that we can play dress-up together. Your new charm will look so pretty on it."

"And I can help, too!" Spike barked. "Speckles can have my old skateboard so we can skate together!"

"Thanks, everyone!" Speckles said.

"What a wonderful Christmas surprise!" Dottie added.

"I realize now that Christmas isn't about gifts," Dottie admitted.

"It's about spending time with the puppies you love!" Speckles agreed. "Merry Christmas, everyone!"